"We must pursue peaceful ends through peaceful means."

—Dr. Martin Luther King Jr.

In honor of those who lost their lives at
Marjory Stoneman Douglas High School,
and those who found their voices
—R. S.

For Will and Eloise—I fight for your more peaceful future—J. A. S.

SIMON & SCHUSTER BOOKS FOR YOUNG READERS
An imprint of Simon & Schuster Children's Publishing Division
1230 Avenue of the Americas, New York, New York 10020
Text copyright © 2018 by Rob Sanders
Illustrations copyright © 2018 by Jared Andrew Schorr
SIMON & SCHUSTER BOOKS FOR YOUNG READERS is a trademark of Simon & Schuster, Inc.
For information about special discounts for bulk purchases, please contact Simon & Schuster Special Sales at
1-866-506-1949 or business@simonandschuster.com.
The Simon & Schuster Speakers Bureau can bring authors to your live event.
For more information or to book an event, contact the Simon & Schuster Speakers Bureau at
1-866-248-3049 or visit our website at www.simonspeakers.com.
The text for this book was set in Century Schoolbook.
The illustrations for this book were rendered in cut paper.
Manufactured in China
0718 SCP
First Edition
2 4 6 8 10 9 7 5 3 1
Library of Congress Cataloging-in-Publication Data
Names: Sanders, Rob, 1958– author. | Schorr, Jared, illustrator.
Title: Peaceful fights for equal rights / Rob Sanders ; Illustrated by Jared Andrew Schorr.
Description: First edition. | New York : Simon & Schuster Books for Young Readers, [2018] | Audience: Age 4 to 8.
| Audience: K to Grade 3.
Identifiers: LCCN 2018006159 (print) | LCCN 2017053165 (eBook)| ISBN 9781534429437 (hardcover)
| ISBN 9781534429444 (eBook)
Subjects: LCSH: Protest movements—Juvenile literature. | Political participation—Juvenile literature.
| Alphabet books.
Classification: LCC HM883 .S26 2018 (eBook) | LCC HM883 (print) | DDC 303.48/4—dc23
LC record available at https://lccn.loc.gov/2018006159

PEACEFUL FIGHTS
for EQUAL RIGHTS

Written by **ROB SANDERS** · Illustrated by **JARED ANDREW SCHORR**

SIMON & SCHUSTER BOOKS FOR YOUNG READERS

NEW YORK   LONDON   TORONTO   SYDNEY   NEW DELHI

Assemble.
Take action.
Create allies.

NOT BOMBS

ENOUGH!

#RESIST
#RESIST
#RESIST

NO MORE WAR

CE
CE

Make buttons.
Make banners.
Make bumper stickers, too.

Boycott!

Boycott!

Boycott!

Chant. Cheer.

Call someone.
Campaign.
Camp out.

Demonstrate.
Don't give up.
Don't give in.

Educate.
Encourage.

IN A GENTLE WAY,
YOU CAN SHAKE THE WORLD.

WHERE THERE IS LOVE,
THERE IS LIFE.

Endure.

Give time. Give strength. Give money if you can.

Shake a hand. Lend a hand. Have hope. Be hope.

Join others on the journey. Join others in the fight.

Knit a hat.

Take a knee.

Listen. Learn. Lead.
Light a candle.
Write a letter.
Pass laws.

March. Mediate.
Meditate. Motivate.

Never sto

Organize. Organize. Organize.

Parade. Picket. Post.

Persist.

Persevere.

Pray.

Ask questions. Never quit.
Quietly do what's right.

Read. Remember.
Resist.

Stand up.
Speak out.
Sit down.
Sing loud.

Be silent.

Turn up the volume.

Unite.

Vote.

Volunteer.

Keep vigil.

Be nonviolent.

Wear it.   Wave it.

Work for it.   Write about it.

Be zealous.

Peaceful Protests

In the 1950s and 1960s, America witnessed nonviolent, peaceful protest on a large scale. The movement was rooted in the philosophies of Henry David Thoreau, who in 1849 wrote the essay "Civil Disobedience." Mahatma Gandhi practiced the principles of non-violence in India in the 1930s, but it was Dr. Martin Luther King Jr. who became well known and well respected as an advocate for the use of peaceful protest in the United States.

In 1957, Dr. King wrote "The Power of Non-violence." Even before that, he had begun teaching about the philosophy of non-violence and using it in protests for African American civil rights. Cesar Chavez used nonviolent protests in the 1960s to organize farmworkers and, later, to gain rights for Hispanics. Those civil rights movements were followed by peaceful anti-war protests and by protests for women's rights, gay rights, the environment, voter rights, and more.

Not all peaceful protests are organized by large groups. When a person votes, he or she might actually be protesting. Sometimes people write a letter to express an opinion, or sing a song of protest, or stop buying certain products or shopping at certain stores, while other people might buy a product to show their support of a particular view. Some might wear a specific T-shirt or button, put a bumper sticker on their car, knit a hat, post on social media, or fly a flag to share their views and opinions in nonviolent ways. Others might light a candle, meditate about positive changes they wish to see, or pray. Some people file lawsuits in the hopes of over-turning laws or creating new ones.

In "The Power of Non-violence" Dr. King explained that the ultimate goal of non-violent protest is not "to humiliate or defeat the opponent but to win his friendship and under-standing." Dr. King said that the outcome of nonviolent protest would be "reconciliation and the creation of a beloved community."

Glossary

assemble [uh-SEHM-buhl]—to gather together in one place

banner [BA-nuhr]—a sign painted on cloth or paper and hung for others to see

boycott [BOI-kaht]—to stop buying or using something, or to stop going to a particular place

bumper sticker [BUHM-puhr STIH-kuhr]—a stick-on piece of paper with a printed message, for sticking to the bumper of a car

button [BUH-tn]—a badge with an image or a printed message; can be pinned on to something else

camp out [KAMP OUT]—to pitch a tent and stay in a location in order to register a protest

campaign [kam-PAYN]—to participate in the competition between candidates for public office

demonstrate [DEH-muhn-strayt]—to gather in order to publicly display a group's feelings toward something

encourage [ehn-KUHR-ij]—to inspire with courage or confidence

endure [ehn-DURE]—to hold out against without yielding

exemplify [ihg-ZEHM-pluh-fie]—to show by example

expect [ihk-SPEKT]—to look forward to

explain [ihk-SPLAYN]—to make something understandable, plain, or clear

imagine [ih-MA-juhn]—to think or believe; to form a mental image of

inform [ihn-FAWRM]—to give knowledge

inquire [ihn-KWIE-uhr]—to seek information; to ask questions

invite [ihn-VITE]—to request the participation or presence of

mediate [MEE-dee-ayt]—to settle disputes

meditate [MEH-duh-tayt]—to contemplate or reflect

nonviolent [non-VIE-uh-luhnt]—peaceful; free of violence

persevere [puhr-suh-VEER]—to persist; to maintain with purpose

persist [puhr-SIST]—to continue on with purpose

picket [PIH-kuht]—to protest with signs during a strike or demonstration

post [POHST]—to publish an online message

resist [rih-ZIST]—to oppose; to withstand; to take a stand

sit down [SIHT DOWN]—or sit in; to participate in a protest where people sit down and will not leave

strike [STRIKE]—to stop work in order to force an employer to comply with demands

take a knee [TAYK ay NEE]—to rest on one knee in protest

unite [yoo-NITE]—to join together

vigil [VIH-juhl]—a period of watchful attention

volunteer [VAW-luhn-teer]—to perform a service willingly and without pay

vote [VOHT]—to use a ballot to express one's opinion or choice

zealous [ZEH-luhs]—filled with passion, enthusiasm, and eagerness